Acder

Russell Punter

Illustrated by David Semple

Adder's starting work today
for Badger's Cleaning Team.

So Adder grabs a ladder,

a bucket

and a cloth.

She checks the first place on her list
and quickly slithers off.

She goes to Hamster's bungalow,
which stands beside the green.

She dunks her cloth in soapy suds...

...and wipes the windows clean.

Parrot Hall is next in line.

The ground floor soon looks fine.

She rests her ladder on the wall
and slowly starts to climb.

Adder's never climbed so high!

Her head begins to spin.

Adder sways
and wobbles.

Her poor heart
starts to pound.

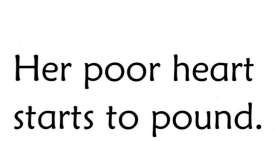

She shuts her eyes up tightly
and slides down to the ground.

"I'm sure to lose my job," she thinks, "if I can't go up higher."

Just then she hears a cry of "HELP!" and spies a house on fire.

Adder doesn't stop to think.
"I'll rescue you!" she shouts.

She wiggles up,
rung after rung...

...and brings
one rabbit out.

Adder rushes up and down,
forgetting all her fears.

"You saved our lives!" the rabbits cry.
The crowd gives her three cheers.

Adder leaves her cleaning job.
Today she firefights.

She's climbing ladders all day long,
now she's not scared of heights.

About phonics

Phonics is a method of teaching reading which is used extensively in today's schools. At its heart is an emphasis on identifying the *sounds* of letters, or combinations of letters, that are then put together to make words. These sounds are known as phonemes.

Starting to read
Learning to read is an important milestone for any child. The process can begin well before children start to learn letters and put them together to read words. The sooner children can discover books and enjoy stories and language, the better they will be prepared for reading themselves, first with the help of an adult and then independently.

You can find out more about phonics on the Usborne Very First Reading website, **usborne.com/veryfirstreading** (US readers go to **veryfirstreading.com**). Click on the **Parents** tab at the top of the page, then scroll down and click on **About synthetic phonics.**

Phonemic awareness

An important early stage in pre-reading and early reading is developing phonemic awareness: that is, listening out for the sounds within words. Rhymes, rhyming stories and alliteration are excellent ways of encouraging phonemic awareness.

In this story, your child will soon identify the *a* sound, as in **Adder** and **ladder.** Look out, too, for rhymes such as **team** – **gleam** and **pound** – **ground.**

Hearing your child read

If your child is reading a story to you, don't rush to correct mistakes, but be ready to prompt or guide if he or she is struggling. Above all, do give plenty of praise and encouragement.

Edited by Jenny Tyler and Lesley Sims
Designed by Sam Whibley and Hope Reynolds

Reading consultants: Alison Kelly and Anne Washtell

First published in 2021 by Usborne Publishing Ltd., Usborne House, 83-85 Saffron Hill, London EC1N 8RT, England.
usborne.com Copyright © 2021 Usborne Publishing Ltd.